Title

Ambient Conditions

Adventures in the Liaden Universe® Number 31

Sharon Lee and Steve Miller

Table of Contents

Thanks

To Mighty Tyop Hunters

Htet Htet Aung, Ronald Currens,

Lloyd Penney, Maurita Plouff

Any typos or infelicities that remain in the text

are the fault of the authors

Copyright Page

Ambient Conditions

Adventures in the Liaden Universe® Number 31

Pinbeam Books: pinbeambooks.com

#

#

"A Visit to the Galaxy Ballroom," was previously published at Baen.com, November 2019. "Ambient Conditions" is original to this chapbook.

#

Cover design by: selfpubbookcovers.com/RLSather

ISBN: 978-1-948465-14-4

Authors' Foreword

or

The Story of the Story

There are two short works included in this chapbook.

The first, "A Visit to the Galaxy Ballroom," is a short story that was previously published to Baen.com in November 2019 in support of the publication of the twenty-second Liaden Universe® novel, *Accepting the Lance.*

The second, "Ambient Conditions," is original to this chapbook. It is a novelette, and a companion story to "Preferred Seating," published to Baen.com in November 2020 in support of the publication of the twenty-third Liaden Universe® novel, *Trader's Leap.*

So, there's a story about "Ambient Conditions."

Understand, there's no proximate reason for this story to exist. It did not demand to be written, as some stories do. It wasn't written to fulfill a contract, or to more fully explore a particular character or situation.

Furthermore, "Ambient Conditions" is a mirror story – which is to say, it's a story we'd already written, told from a different point of view. Now, we *do* like to play with viewpoints at scene-length – Val Con and Miri being described as cute kids by people who have no clue who they're looking at is always good for a chuckle, for instance.

But we don't write *whole stories* over again; it makes us feel a little uneasy, as if we're cheating.

So, why *did* you write this story, we hear you ask.

Well, it's like this ...

Between handing in *Trader's Leap* late in 2019, and its publication late in 2020, Sharon had a mastectomy. As such things go, it was ... not as bad as it could have been, but not much fun, either. In fact, it was a life-changing event. And life-changing events tend to take up all available processing space for quite a while. Not only was it necessary to endure and survive the physical insults of the amputation and the following radiation treatments, but there were meetings with doctors, and with PAs, and with more doctors; instructions to follow, meds to adjust to, and, and ...

Long story short – Sharon forgot how to write. Not how to write sentences – she updated her blog and was pretty active on Facebook – but how to write *fiction*, which is an operation far, far more complex than merely writing sentences.

It was, particularly, the *movement* part of writing a story that was giving Sharon the most trouble, which she discovered after an abortive attempt to write a story set in her Carousel universe, and another attempt to write backstory for Kasagaria Mikelsyn, and yet a third attempt – well.

After the third attempt, she realized that she was going to have to deconstruct the process, and relearn how to write, one facet at a time.

This was when she hit upon the idea of using a story that had already been written as a pattern. She knew the plot, and the characters, and how the story ended. All she had to do was tell over the same action, from the point of view of the second main character in the story.

If that didn't work, she told Steve gloomily, she'd have to resort to retyping a story – or a novel – until her brain got on the case again.

Happily, retelling "Preferred Seating" from Kishara's point of view *was* the cure, and as of this writing, Sharon pronounces herself a graduate of the Relearning to Write curriculum.

We hope you enjoy the stories in this chapbook.

Sharon Lee and Steve Miller

Cat Farm and Confusion Factory

December 2020

A Visit to the Galaxy Ballroom

Scout Lina yo'Bingim inhaled, tasting the sharp, cold air, feeling a phantom flutter against her cheek. She blinked up at the gray sky, at snow – snow! She paid off the cabbie, soft flakes melting against her face.

She liked the fresh smell of the snow, but she had not come here to linger in quiet appreciation on the street. No, her purpose was to have a good time, while enthusiastically expending energy.

Scout Lina yo'Bingim, off-duty for the next twenty-four hours, turned away from the curb, and walked determinedly toward the building with the message lit up in bright pink and yellow lights:

WELCOME TO THE GALAXY BALLROOM

According to her information, she would find Scouts and pilots and mercenaries inside. She would find dancing, and gaming, and drinking, and – bowli ball.

She had specifically come for the bowli ball.

Inside the bar was everything one might expect of a rowdy emporium on a deep space route: twenty-three kinds of beer and ale instabrewed on the premises; both top-line and bottom-tier liquor, but none in-between; and wine in quantity. A modest line of smokes was also on offer, for those who sought peace.

Peace was not what Lina had come for.

Ten Standard Days ago, she had been on Liad, and looking forward with warm anticipation to Festival, at Solcintra. It had been a very difficult year; she deserved the Festival and she had intended to take full benefit from all of the festivities open to her.

Nine Standard Days ago, she had been called in to her commander's office–and given a mission.

She was to transport the Council-appointed Administrative Arbiter of Scouts, one Chola as'Barta, to Surebleak in the Daiellen Sector with "all haste." She was detached from her usual duties to this mission; with Chola as'Barta her immediate superior and supervisor.

She was assigned *Bentokoristo*, she being one of six to have trained on it–a new ship sporting a not-quite-experimental enhanced drive, and an upgraded weapons system.

That was sole piece of good news; *Bentokoristo* was beautiful to fly. But no matter how fast the ship was, she was not fast enough to get to Surebleak and back again in time for the Festival at Solcintra, even if Lina flew like a Scout – which was not, after all, an option.

Admin as'Barta was ... not a Scout. Lina was therefore constrained to put together a series of Jumps which would get them from Solcintra to Surebleak with a minimum of downtime, and which would not strain the resources of a man who counted five trips to the gaming salons in Liad's orbit as being an experienced space traveler. Admin as'Barta must, the commander insisted, arrive in fit condition, able to immediately embark upon his mission. The Administrator had been appointed to find what had occasioned the schism of the Scouts on Surebleak, creating the foolish situation of two Scout organizations – the Liaden Scouts, and the so-called Surebleak Scouts.

Nine Standard Days, the trip had taken, coddling Admin as'Barta.

For his part, he ignored her advice to move onto Surebleak time before they arrived, and periodically infringed on her rest shifts to try to talk the politics of the fissioning Scouts. He'd asked her why she thought the break had occurred, and her reply – "pilot's choice" – had satisfied him not at all.

And, there, he *wasn't* a Scout, he was a Council-appointee, selected for his supposed "connections" in the piloting sphere. It was unlikely he'd known anyone who had died at Nev'Lorn, nor was he aware of the treachery that had led to the battle there.

"But how," he had demanded, as they waited for dinner to warm, "could a Liaden, born and bred to excellence in all things, having achieved a place in life through being a Scout – how could any such person turn their back on Liad and all that Liad offers? Liadens have the advantage of the Code and delms for guidance!"

"The same reason, Admin. A pilot flies the best course they may with the information to hand. A pilot operates in the moment, with the delm light years away and the Code irrelevant to the case."

"Have you found the Code irrelevant on many occasions, pilot?"

He held up a hand, forestalling a reply she had not intended to make.

"Consider your answer carefully. I will be needing an assistant after I am approved as permanent Director of Scout Operations on Surebleak. Once I have spoken to ter'Meulen, and this foolish matter has been regularized, there will be many rewarding administrative tasks available to a discerning Scout who may wish promotion and increased *melant'i*."

At that point, the chime sounded for dinner being hot and ready, and Lina had deftly avoided the topic of promotion to as'Barta's assistant. As to the "foolish matter" of the schism – if it was *Clonak ter'Meulen* with whom the Admin was to liaise, then the matter would be settled by tea-time. One could, if one wished, wonder why the most devious Scout currently serving hadn't fixed the "foolish matter" already, but that was merely a waste of time. Clonak always had his reasons, though they be ever so inobvious.

At last, they had made Surebleak, and she was granted leave – twenty-four hours free of Admin as'Barta! – but not before she had been instructed as to proper behavior even on her own time.

"Do not fraternize with the locals, Scout. Beware of any attempts to make you divulge your mission. I am told that there are places where proper Scouts meet. You will confine yourself to those venues."

Repairing to the small room she had been granted, Lina called up the screen and considered her options.

Given the connection to Clan Korval and their likely inclusion of the vague and detested "locals," she decided not to attempt the Emerald Casino. The entertainments advertised at Audrey's House of Joy tempted, but again, there would likely be "locals" present.

Best Bowli Ball Court on Surebleak! the next advertisement promised, and Lina grinned. She did consider the "local" angle, but reasoned such an emporium more likely to attract Scouts than Admin's loose "locals."

Lina therefore called a cab, and very shortly she was entering The Galaxy Ballroom.

She stopped at the counter to buy a ticket – not, alas, a token for a private Festival bower, or a key to an all-night playroom – but admission as a contestant in one bout of "real bowli ball action!" which would at least warm her blood and satisfy her need for action, if not her wistful libido.

She excused her way past several inebriated mercs, one a red-haired master sergeant who briefly thought she'd come for him alone, but then he recognized the jacket and insignia and bowed a polite, "Efning, pilot!" at her hopefully. "Come back if you need a winner!"

He'd managed to grab a table and was large enough that it was mostly hidden behind him. "I got two chairs, prezzels, a warm heart – and I just been paid!"

She gathered that he did have a warm heart – her empathy rating was just below that qualifying as a small talent – but she'd been considering a real workout, and soon.

She smiled, and her hand flung an equally polite *busy here* in his direction as she moved into the darkness, seeking that proper bowli ball deck, with transparent walls and resilient ceiling, an excellent air system, and opponents worthy of her.

Half-dozen languages brushed past her ears; the potent scent of alcohol mixed with the additional odors of many dozens of people exuding sweat and energy in the dimness.

Ahead, she heard a distant thud, and another, a round of cheers and laughter, a high voice calling, "I'll still take two to one on the blue boots!"

Scout skill to the fore, Lina yo'Bingim slid between two hefty mercs on their sudden way to the john as yes – there!

There were four players on the deck, their time almost up. She stopped to watch the play.

One player stood out. He was doing too many dives to stay in the game much longer; in the mirrored ceiling, she could see him rolling to his feet with an awkward re-step to gain his balance. She could tell that he was hurting – it didn't take her high empathy rating or her training in body language across three cultures to see that.

She pushed forward, the better to see the clock.

Ah, that was the key. He had only seconds to hit his mark ... and finish, at least.

The ball came at him again; he kneed it roughly, it went higher than his other knee, which had likely not been his intent, but he made a good recovery by striking it with his elbow, the ball's own kinetics giving it an off-centered boost in the direction of the oldest fellow on the deck, who nonchalantly elbowed it on to a third person who –

Blangblangblang!

The bell rang; the third and fourth in the action dove for the ball together and came up laughing, bobbling the thing back and forth as it tried to spend the energy gained from the last burst of action. The spectators cheered, money changed hands, and the transparent door to the deck was opened as the next players moved forward.

The MC spoke purposefully into the mic, "Next up we have a five-group, came in together, and then ..."

The player who had overexerted himself stumbled as he left the court, was steadied briefly by another of the combatants with an over-wide grin ... and collapsed on the spot, nose bleeding.

"I'm a medic," one of the group entering the court yelled, and one of his companions added – "field medics, here, let us through!"

That quickly, the downed player was off the floor, and the next group of players, as well. The Master of Ceremonies looked around, eyes bright, and spoke into the mic.

"Hold up your tickets, show your cards! We'll do a quick single-match to give the next group time to get back!"

Lina's arm reached high – yellow ticket, solo ...

The MC saw her, waved her toward the deck door and pointed at another yellow –

"Come on up, pilots! Now or never; we got group play booked 'til after midnight!"

They met on the court, her opponent near her own age, a pilot, and, she saw with pleasure, a Scout. He wore light duty clothes, no rank marks visible, save the wings on his collar; his face was open, and a hint of a smile showing.

He would do, thought Lina, and returned the smile.

"Well, pilot?" she challenged him. "Shall we?"

He took a moment to survey her – she saw his eyes catch on the wings adorning her own collar, before he bowed, Scout to Scout.

"Pilot, we shall!"

"All right!" the MC called. "Let's get the ball rolling! Twelve minute match – what'll it be?" he asked, turning to them. "Liaden training rules, Scout standard rules, open court rules?"

"Scout standard?" she asked her opponent, and got a flicker of fingers in agreement.

"I am Lina," she said, stripping off her jacket and giving it into the MC's ready hand.

"Kelby," he answered, also relinquishing his jacket.

"Check the equipment, Pilots, you got thirty-three seconds."

Kelby received the ball first to check. Lina ran a quick rainbow, for focus, and looked about her.

"Spot!" she called, pointing, as Kelby called out, "Here also!"

The MC waved; a younger with a mop rushed onto court and dealt with the spot of sweat, and the other, of blood.

"Right!" the MC shouted into his mic. "Up here we got Kelby and Lina, pickup match, twelve minutes, Scout standard!"

The crowd cheered, briefly.

The MC turned to them.

"Any private challenge; any bet between the two of you?"

Kelby looked at her, hands raised, face glowing as if he'd already been playing five minutes ...

Lina bent forward, as eager as he to get the match started, whispering:

"Loser buys both breakfast?"

A grin showed in brief appreciation; she saw interest in his eyes.

He bowed, formally, accepting the challenge of an equal, and repeated the stakes to the MC, who outright laughed.

"All right, soldiers and pilots! Scouts and citizens! These two know how the game is played! Got a little private bet going – loser buys breakfast for both!"

The cheering this time was fuller, longer; the bell went *blangblangblang*; the MC slammed the bowli ball into the circle between them, and dove for the safety of the transparent observer's booth.

\#

The deck was better than Lina had anticipated. The floor gave a firm, even footing without being loud; it was resilient rather than bouncy. She and Kelby had almost overrun each other on the launch, but the spin favored Lina. She twisted to catch and flick the busy ball high off a wall behind Kelby.

From within, the walls were slightly smoky and even ball-streaked, but her first corner fling proved they were in good condition.

The first several minutes were given to testing – the facility, the ball, each other. The ball was regulation, with a tricky underspin. Every fifth or sixth time it hit, the ball added rather than subtracted and the amplified spin could push it along the wall or out of a grasping hand.

The match being timed rather than one-and-out, they both survived learning the ball's eccentricities; Lina first when the ball tore itself from her hand to bounce down her wrist and into her chest, much to the delight of the crowd, and Kelby who'd timed a leap-and-grab perfectly, displaying both great style and interesting physique, only to have the ball hang for a half-second longer than anticipated, before flinging itself across the surface of the wall like a hurrying caterpillar.

The bell *blanged* caution at six minutes; distracted, Kelby had to do a three-hit, elbow, shoulder, palm to get the ball where he wanted it for his next throw. Between them, they'd been upping the tempo, and both still taking time to observe each other's moves and strengths.

Yes, Lina thought; he'll do *nicely*, as he turned from the recover and threw unexpectedly over his shoulder with his back to her – a good view – nearly rooting her to the spot with the trick move. She deflected the ball with her ankle before it hit the floor, portions of the betting crowd apparently doubtful that she'd managed it, and then had to dive and kick with the other foot, but this was one of *her* tricks, angling the ball high off the wall, against the ceiling, and onto another wall, the ball underspinning, leaving Kelby little choice but to do a dive of his own and juggle the ball until he mastered the tempo sufficiently to get his footwork back in sync.

"One each, here at the center stage!" called the MC. "Get your bets in, watch the action! Winner gets a free breakfast 'cause the loser's going to pay! Thrills and chills here – Hey! Didja see that recover?"

Lina took the next throw with her left hand and did a quick launch; Kelby barely had time to catch and do the same. For several moments, they traded the ball at throat level – flick, flick, flick–eyes on the ball, the throat, the face, slowly coming closer, faster ...

Their eyes locked briefly as they trusted the motion, then they began backing away as they continued the same throw and catch at least a dozen more times. He changed it up: took the ball left-handed and swung back and around once before launching vertically so Lina had to move closer to catch it.

It was her turn to vary, her throw bouncing off a sidewall so she could catch it, and she did that twice again, moving toward a corner, making him retreat to stay in front of her. Then an underhanded lob toward the leg he'd just raised and ...

A roll! He landed hard, snatched the ball, the roll brought him very close before the ball was released, and he used the wall for the save, the angle bouncing the ball from wall to ceiling.

It was the ceiling that almost defeated her; Lina managing to just get to the bounce that extended to the other side of Kelby, who was still rising. The ball was in overdrive. Lina lunged, got a hand on it, and then tangled in Kelby's legs, the ball bouncing overhead, with the crowd roaring.

Kelby lunged from his spot in the tangle, keeping the ball up, and she did the same, on one knee, as he reached through her arms and swung to keep it higher; the continued nearness a surprise, the joint effort promising.

The crowd was cheering wildly, some counting, and the "four, three, two, one ..." ended with the *blangblandblang* of the closing bell.

Lina smothered the ball, hand on her shoulder to keep it still while Kelby's hand was also on her shoulder, and a laughing MC made his way onto the deck ...

"Looks like we gotta live heat here! Even score! Guess the pilots here'll hafta figure out who pays for breakfast some other way, hey?"

He reached cautiously for the ball, with Kelby and Lina not quite smoothly working it from between them into his hand.

"I tell you what," he said into the mic, working the still merry crowd. "This ball's had quite a workout – it's still buzzing and so am I! Big cheer for Lina and Kelby!"

The crowd obliged as the MC helped the two of them finish detangling, and the mop-up crew came in to make all seemly for the next group.

"You're good," Lina told Kelby as they hurried out, jackets in hand.

He bowed on the move, hand rising to sign *So are you.*

"I'm just in today," she said, when they paused by the door to pull on their jackets. "Please, Pilot, lead on!"

#

Lina returned to port with an hour still to run on her leave. The room she had been assigned was scarcely more than a pilot's ready room: a cot, some shelves, and a screen.

Kelby's rooms were multiple and tidy, the small kitchen, small bath, and small living area with both a couch and a bed far wider than a cot.

As it came about, she had paid for breakfast at Reski's, a mere three hundred paces from his rooms – perfectly equitable, as he had paid the taxi, shared his wine and worthy snacks, and not the least, his bed.

This room – well. If she were to be on Surebleak longer than three nights, she would have to find something else.

But that was for later. For now, her condition was considerably improved.

She'd had a romp far better than an impromptu Festival meeting, and had already accumulated a favorite morning café, taxi company, and bowli ball court, not to mention having Scout Lieutenant Kelby chel'Vona Clan Nosko's personal and work comm codes in her pocket.

Came the sound of steps in the hall, followed by imperious knocking and the querulous voice of her direct superior.

"Open now, yo'Bingim!"

For a heartbeat, she considered ignoring the command, her leave with yet an hour to run.

"yo'Bingim!"

She growled softly, and stepped to the door, opening with hairbrush in one hand and in the other, her wings.

Administrator as'Barta stood in the door, a pilot Lina had never seen before behind him – she was not a Scout.

"So you returned after making your contact, did you? I had word that you were off in the wilds beyond the city last night."

Lines of anger bracketed his mouth.

Mastering her own spurt of anger, Lina bowed a brief welcome to her superior, and made no answer regarding her whereabouts while on leave.

"Should you like to come in, Administrator?"

"No, I should not, yo'Bingam. Give me the key cards for our ship – all that are in your possession."

"All," she repeated, unsnapping her pouch even as she turned toward her jacket, hung on the back of a chair.

"You will not need your jacket," as'Barta snapped.

"A pilot keeps keys to hand, sir. You had wanted all in my possession."

She slipped her hand into the discreet inner pocket and removed the first set of keys, and the second set from her pouch. Those she brought to the door, and held toward the Administrator, who fell back a step and waved peremptorily at the stranger pilot.

"Pilot sig'Sted receives the keys."

The pilot stepped forward to do so, her eyes averted. Lina frowned at the logo on the breast of her jacket. vee'Mastin Lines, she saw.

Administrator as'Barta's vaunted "connections with the piloting sphere" included owning half of vee'Mastin Lines.

Lina's fingers tightened on the keys, and she pulled them slightly back.

"I will surrender these to a Scout," she said. "vee'Mastin Lines has no cause to hold the keys to a Scout ship."

"You will surrender those keys when and to whom I direct you!" snarled as'Barta. "Give them to her!"

"No," said Lina, and put both sets of keys into her pouch.

"Insubordination! I will see you stripped of rank, and license."

"I will surrender the keys of a Scout ship to a Scout," Lina returned. "You have hundreds of Scouts at your beck, Administrator. Call one here."

He moved, suddenly, surprisingly, kicking at her knee. She jumped back, avoiding the clumsy blow – and the door closed with a snap that meant the outside lock had been engaged.

Lina crossed the room to her screen, and called the duty desk.

"This is Lina yo'Bingam. I need to schedule an appointment with the base commander, immediately," she said.

There was a pause.

"Lina yo'Bingam, you are already on the commander's hearing list," the duty desk officer said. "Administrative Arbiter of Scouts as'Barta has filed a complaint, and placed your license under lock. The hearing is scheduled in two hours. You will be escorted to the meeting room."

#

Escort had been two Scout security officers. They had checked her weapon, locked it, and allowed her to return it to its place in her jacket. Ship keys were not mentioned; the first set was in her jacket; the second set in her pouch – standard procedure. Lina walked between her escorts calmly, eager to lay the situation out before a Scout, who knew the regs, and who would understand her objection to turning over the keys to a Scout ship to a passenger line pilot.

Her escort triggered the release on a door, and she walked into the conference room between them.

Before her was a conference table. Behind the conference table was Admin as'Barta, a hard-faced Scout captain – and the passenger line pilot to whom she had refused to give *Bentokoristo's* keys.

There were no chairs on her side of the table.

Lina drew a hard breath.

"Why is there a civilian at this Scout hearing?" she asked.

"It is not your place to ask questions here," snapped Admin as'Barta.

The Scout captain frowned.

"I will answer. It is a reasonable question of protocol, and an unusual situation."

He inclined his head slightly.

"Pilot sig'Sted is Administrator as'Barta's advising pilot. As the difficulties the Administrator has come to solve are Scout-based, it is considered best that the Administrator's team be outside of the Scout hierarchy."

"The disciplinary hearing is now called to order," Admin said briefly. "This procedure is being recorded and will become part of your permanent records."

He glanced down at his tablet and began speaking in her direction without making eye contact. As he spoke, he ran his fingers down the tablet, apparently checking tick-boxes as he hit each point.

"Last evening I had dinner with Pilot sig'Sted, a mature pilot well-known to me. Her *melant'i* is without stain, and I trust her implicitly in all matters of piloting."

Pilot sig'Sted, seated next to him had the grace to look embarrassed.

Lina put her hands behind her back, and broadened her stance, waiting.

"I described to Pilot sig'Sted the irregular and exhausting journey produced by Scout yo'Bingam on my behalf. Pilot sig'Sted gave it as her professional opinion that the pilot in charge had been hasty and foolhardy, had made questionable and potentially dangerous choices of route, and subjected me to unnecessary hardship."

He paused to glance up, but did not meet Lina's eyes.

"Based on this information, I immediately moved to have Scout yo'Bingim's license revoked until she has taken remedial piloting classes and re-certifies at every level."

Lina looked at the Scout Captain.

He avoided her eyes.

"I am," she said, "a Scout pilot. That is the equivalent of a *master pilot*. I –"

"You do yourself no good by being uncooperative," Admin as'Barta stated.

The Scout Captain said nothing.

Lina bit her lip.

"In addition to her piloting errors, and willful disrespect for my person, my *melant'i*, and my office, it has become clear that Lina yo'Bingim is an agent of the false Scouts. No sooner had we landed, she filed for leave, and met with an agent attached to the command structure of the very group which I am here to correct and bring back into alignment with the proper Liaden Scouts.

"In short, Lina yo'Bingim is working against my office, my mission, and myself. She is working to undermine and destroy the Liaden Scouts! Revoking her license to fly scarcely begins to address the problem. She must be struck from the lists of Liaden Scouts. In this, she will finally serve my office and my mission, by standing as an example of what happens to those who work against the proper order and the Code."

"Scout Captain – " Lina began.

"Be silent," Admin as'Barta snapped.

She glared at him, felt her escort shift closer from the sides, and closed her eyes briefly, accessing the rainbow, for calmness.

"You may retain your place in the Scouts, though at a much reduced rank," Admin as'Barta said, then. "Tell me what information you shared with this agent of the schismatic officer ter'Meulen."

She took a breath.

"He named his ship; I named mine. We shared our class years and first flight dates. We counted the bruises we had from the bowli ball match we had played, and laughed because there, too, we had tied. I did not tell him the name of my superior; he did not tell me the name of his, though ter'Meulen – "

She looked again to the Scout Captain, who did not meet her eye.

"ter'Meulen," she continued, facing the admin again, "was head of pilot security for the Scouts – for the *Liaden* Scouts – for decades. He is no enemy of yours. If it is *ter'Meulen* who has authored this breach, then you must look for the fault in our own ranks."

Admin as'Barta sat back, satisfied. He turned to the Scout Captain.

"You hear her. She must be cast out."

"Yes," the Scout Captain said. "I hear her. The paperwork will be completed this afternoon."

"Captain," Lina said urgently. "The keys to the Scout ship I piloted here – *Bentokoristo*. There are only six trained to fly her ..."

"That is no longer your concern, Lina yo'Bingim," he told her, and held out his hand.

"The keys, if you please."

Relief almost undid her. At least, in this, he would be proper. The Scout ship would be relinquished to a Scout.

She reached into her jacket, into her pouch, approached the table and placed the keys in his hand.

"Escort, take Lina yo'Bingim to her quarters. Hold yourselves ready to escort her out of this facility, once the paperwork is complete. Dismissed."

#

She was a Scout; everything she needed or wanted was in her jacket. Her license ... she drew it out, slid it into the slot – and caught it when it was forcibly spat out – rejected.

Thoughtfully, she considered Admin as'Barta, the Council of Clans, and the assumptions surrounding this mission to re-unite the Scouts.

She then considered Clonak ter'Meulen, whom she had known, slightly. A Scout sublime, Clonak ter'Meulen, and one who cared for his pilots above all other things.

What could have happened, to make Clonak ter'Meulen break away from the Scouts he had loved?

The door to her cubicle opened. Her escort said, "It is time."

They handed her a stick – her records, they said. They walked her to the door, and outside, into the port. They left her standing on cold 'crete at the edge of the street, and went back inside.

Lina yo'Bingim inhaled sharply, tasting the sharp, cold air, feeling the phantom flutter of a snowflake against her cheek.

Across the way, she saw the bright green of a call-box. She crossed to it, fingering the slip of paper with Kelby chel'Vona's numbers on it out of her belt.

He answered at once, sounding pleased to hear from her so soon.

"I find we have an acquaintance in common," she said, after they had been pleased with each other. "Clonak ter'Meulen."

"Yes, of course. Everyone knows Clonak, so I've always heard it."

"I, too," she said. "He never let a pilot reside in peril. I wonder if you could bring me to him?"

"Certainly, but – why?"

"One of the things I recall Clonak saying – his fondness for Terran quotations, you know. He had used to quite often say that *It's better to be part of the solution than part of the problem.*

"I want to talk to him about becoming part of the solution."

Ambient Conditions

"Oh," Kishara's younger sister Troodi said as she opened the door and beheld her elder sitting in the chair by the window, a book on her knee.

"Oh," Troodi said again, her eyes filling with tears. "Shara, I thought that – I'd *hoped that* – you'd – gone ahead."

"As you see, I am here," Kishara said gently, putting the book aside and rising. That she'd leave clan and kin ahead of this, her delm's summons to a banishment – but where would she have gone? She might, perhaps, have fled to *Maplekai*, had it been in port, but such a move would have endangered Clan Monfit entire. The Council in its current mood was perfectly capable of seizing her family's tradeship in Balance of an attempt to escape its instructions. And to hide on Liad – well, there was only the Low Port, and no one's dreams survived there.

She did not say these things to her sister, who was not yet halfling, and could only see their uncle's betrayal. Later, when she was older, and, one hoped, her life less imperiled–then she would see that this had been the only course that would have preserved the clan, which was the duty of a delm. To Troodie, at twelve, it must seem there were no limits on the delm's power.

Kishara, her elder by a dozen Standards, had no fault to find with the delm's actions to preserve the clan, though she might have wished for a small sign or token to demonstrate an uncle's regard for the niece he must sacrifice, but there, Uncle Bry Sen had scarcely emerged from the delm, or the delm from his office, since the decision had at last been taken.

"This," Troodi said abruptly, her voice warm with hope; "Kishara, *surely* this proves them wrong? How is this moment lucky for you? How, therefore, are you *lucky beyond nature?*"

Her gift – the talent that made her a despised outcast – was at the best of times too strange to explain to one not similarly burdened. Still, one could not leave a young sister utterly without comfort. Kishara folded Troodi into an embrace.

"Sometimes," she murmured, her dry cheek pressed against her sister's damp one. "Sometimes, what seems at first to be the blackest bad luck is found, after a passage of time, and a re-examination of circumstance, to have been the best luck possible."

Her sister sniffled.

"Is this one of those times?" she asked, her tone, rightly, doubtful.

Kishara held her at arm's length, and produced a smile that was not wholly false.

"That we cannot know, until we allow time to pass."

She bent and kissed her sister's cheek.

"I must go," she said. "Try to forgive Uncle Bry Sen, sweeting; he's never so fierce as you are. And the delm – why, the delm has no choice in this at all, if he would protect the greater part of Monfit's treasures. This is not over, I'll wager. Your ferocity will be needed on behalf of the clan, yet."

Her sister considered her, face bearing an expression between wariness and hope.

"Do you – do you *know* that?" she asked.

Kishara thought about those things that had produced this moment, when all of those in possession of small talents were held away from joining with the Healers in their guildhall, were declared dangers to society and to the homeworld, and ordered to submit to sterilization, execution, or banishment.

There had been a certain amount of genuine fear in the discovery that there were *so many* "unregulated talents" present in the general population, for there are always those who fear what they fail to understand. But there had also been greed – for some clans would lose too many, and they would be easy meat for those who were ruled by avarice.

So, then, thought Kishara; the truth for Troodi, so that she might stand strong and vigilant for the clan.

"Yes," said Kishara firmly. "I *know* that you will be needed."

There were footsteps heard then, down the end of the hall, moving rapidly closer. Kishara turned to pick up her jacket.

She kissed her sister's cheek again before opening the door to reveal her cousin Ern Din's frowning face.

"Come," she said briskly, stepping 'round him. "It is time for me to go."

* * *

Perhaps it was spite. Perhaps it was expediency. Perhaps it was, as they said, honest horror to find a dire threat to the purity of Liaden society living, all unrecognized, among them.

However it became known, and for whatever reason it was pursued, the Council of Clans had, by majority vote – Korval and Ixin, Justus and Deshnol the four clans who stood against – decreed that all clans give up such members who exhibited abilities which were known to be out of the common way, whether the delm deemed them dangerous or not.

The penalty for withholding such persons was to be written out of the Book of Clans, which threat was immediately implemented, to the sorrow of Clan-Natis-that-was, which had long been a thorn in the side of the Council. It had been a thorough breaking, with the delm, both thodelms, and their heirs sent to outworlds as bonded laborers, while those others of Natis who were deemed "untainted" were acquired by such houses that had need to boost their numbers. The two found to possess abilities out of the common way were put to death, the Council disallowing the delm her right to perform the act herself.

Though she had been required to watch.

Having administered this terrible lesson, the Council may have been confident that delms would act as delms must – to preserve the greater good, and the greater numbers, of their clans.

But even frightened delms could not bring themselves to surrender their children – innocent of any wrongdoing save being odd – to death. Delm spoke to delm, there was talk – much talk – regarding what *melant'i* required, and more talk yet regarding the Code, and what might fall outside of civilized behavior.

There had been consternation in the halls of the Council. There had been shouting and threats. The Council offered a compromise – the odd ones would not be murdered, but merely sterilized so their abnormal genes died with them.

Into this second wave of outrage stepped Clan Korval, who had been instrumental in creating the Healers Guild, some years gone by. Korval suggested that the abnormal – which in gentle courtesy they named "small talents" – be brought into the Healers Guild, and trained in the forms of that House. Thus affiliated, they would be neither surprise nor threat.

The Council ordered the Accountants Guild, who had drawn up the charter for the Healers, to find if Korval's suggested solution had merit.

It was said that the *qe'andra* who stood before the Council to report the results of research wept openly as he gave the opinion of the experts: None but those who displayed the talents detailed in the charter, those talents acknowledged as being on the *Healer Spectrum* might join the Guild. No provision had been made in the charter for other, or different, styles of talent. The advice of the Accountants Guild was that the Healer's Guild amend their charter, or that another charter be drawn up, forming a guild which would protect those talents not found to be on the *Healer Spectrum*. He had added, into the silence that greeted this report, that the Accountants Guild would be pleased to assist in either project, pro bono.

Speaker for Council ruled the discussion of amended charters and new Guilds off-topic, and was on the edge of calling for a vote on the issue of nullifying the threat posed by the abnormal, but Korval was up again, demanding that each and all of the small talents be tested by the Healers, so that those who were found to be on the *Healer Spectrum* could properly be brought into the Guild.

The demand was reasonable; the Council could not gainsay it, though it could and did set a tight deadline.

So, the small talents were tested.

Kishara herself had come close – quite *improbably* close, to her mind – to achieving the *Healer Spectrum* on the strength of her second small talent. The testing Healer, all honor to him, had insisted on a second examination, by a master of the Guild. The master found her gift too erratic to be of use to the House. Even then, the testing Healer had asserted that she might well improve with training; that they were none of them born in perfect control of their gifts, that –

He had been silenced then by the Council-appointed witness, even as Kishara had whispered to *let be*, lest he suddenly be discovered to have no aptitude for Healing, and was in addition a danger to the general population.

It was said that three of the many tested were found to be on the Healer Spectrum. The rest – were once again championed by Clan Korval and their allies.

They offered those small talents who did not wish to remain on the homeworld at the price of their future children the opportunity to emigrate to a world seeking colonists, well away from Liad, and far from the oversight of the Council of Clans. Clan Korval and Clan Ixin between them would supply transport.

* * *

They were counted off in twelves as they came aboard, the twelfth given a tablet, which displayed orders and information. The tablet-holder of Kishara's group was a woman who gave her name simply as Pritti, with neither Line nor clan to distinguish her further, who asked their names, and ticked them off on the screen. That done, she guided them to a pod of twelve acceleration couches placed kin-close near the end of a short hallway.

They settled in their own order, with Kishara on Pritti's left, which earned her a smile and a question.

"What is your talent?"

"I am found to be too fortunate," she said promptly. "And you?"

"I can tell who has touched an object only by touching it myself."

Kishara frowned.

"That sounds – rather useful," she said, then caught herself up. "Your pardon."

"No need." Pritti smiled. "It *is* rather useful, as it happens, merely it is not on the Healer Spectrum. Also, my cousin Ihana has secrets to keep, and has long wished me away."

She glanced beyond Kishara, and spoke to the elder reclining on the next couch.

"And your talent, sir?"

"I can weave rainbows." He moved a wrinkled hand in an arc above his face, as he lay there.

Colors glowed against the air, following the pattern his hand described. He made a fist, and the dainty thing lingered for a moment before fading coyly away.

"Where is the harm in that?" demanded Kishara.

The elder laughed softly and said, "Not on the Healer Spectrum."

"Indeed." Pritti turned to the couch on her right, where a man of no particular distinction sat, feet firmly on the decking.

"What is your talent, Mor Gan?"

"I?" He lifted a shoulder, and let it fall. "I – make suggestions."

It was said easily enough, but Kishara shivered where she lay, propped on one elbow.

"Suggest *what sort* of things," Pritti asked, sharp enough that Kishara knew she was not alone in being discomfited.

"Well, I might suggest that you give me that silver ring on your finger," he said, and there was *some*thing there, in the cadence of his words. Pritti raised a hand on which silver flashed brightly. She raised her other hand, as if she would have the ornament off. Kishara held her breath even as the other woman hesitated.

"No," Pritti said, firmly, and folded her hands together in her lap.

The man – Mor Gan – laughed.

"And there you have it," he said, his voice easy again, "perfectly useless. However, it *is* disquieting, which is why my delm cast me out before even the Council's recent start."

"Cast you out?" said the elder. "Where did you go, then?"

"Oh, to Low Port," said Mor Gan, and there, again, was *that* note in his voice. "A man might profit there, if he takes good counsel and aligns himself well."

"And yet," Pritti said, "you did not choose to stay on Liad, though you were so well-situated."

There was a smile in his voice this time.

"I had always wished to see other worlds, and it scarcely seemed that a like offer would come my way again."

There was an uneasy silence. Pritti had raised her head to address the couch beyond, when there came a loud click, which might have been, Kishara thought, from the all-ship comm. In another moment, this theory was confirmed by a voice speaking in the mode of pilot to passengers.

"All passengers, this is Grasa ven'Deelin Clan Ixin, pilot and first board. We will be lifting within the next hour. Allow me to regret the conditions in which you are constrained to undertake this journey. Our purpose was to accommodate as many as we might without endangering either the ship or its passengers. In keeping with these goals, we will be introducing a soporific into the air supply. The journey will pass more quickly for you, and you will consume less supplies. By reducing the amount of rations we must carry, we were able to accommodate three more passengers.

"Those who were given tablets upon boarding are the leaders of your twelve-group. Each group will be waked according to the schedule now on the screen. Leaders will at those times check on the well-being of the group, and see that each partakes of the nutrients provided. Again, allow me to regret these conditions. The pilots swear that we will go as quickly as possible, and will deliver you safely into circumstances far better than those you are leaving."

There was some exclamation, and a very modest amount of disturbance, due, Kishara thought, lying back on her couch, to the drug that had doubtless been introduced into the air supply some time ago.

She sighed, and closed her eyes, and deliberately took deep breaths until sleep swept her away.

* * *

It was a strange sleep, full with chaotic events and odd people, and her brief wakings scarcely more sensible. She was given a hard bar to eat and something thick and vile-tasting to drink, marched to the necessary, and back to the couch, where the dreams took her again between one blink and another.

There was, she thought, at one waking, an empty couch, which had been the elder's. She had stopped there, struck with something that might have been sorrow, had she been awake enough to process the emotion.

"It was only a pretty thing he did, and no harm to it," she'd said, and Pritti – perhaps it was Pritti – made some answer that she forgot as soon as she'd heard it.

The dreams became ever more mysterious, salted with a sense of danger, and one face, seen often – a hard face, set in displeasure, well-marked brows pulled tight over dark eyes, mouth straight and tight.

There was something attached to that face – some sort of urgency that tasted of her gift. She sought that face, tried to tarry nearby when she found it, but she had no control, no technique, and the other images crowded her away, confusing her with their multitudes.

Then, the dreams stopped.

"Kishara," someone said. "Kishara, wake now. We are arrived."

* * *

They were a motley crowd of supplicants, to be sure, thin and pale and not a little anxious. Kishara might have found it in her to think hardly of their supposed rescuers, saving that the pilots came on-screen to explain procedures going forward, and it could be seen that they were not one whit less worn than their passengers.

"The Office of Colonization has long expected our arrival," Pilot ven'Deelin said. "There are certain examinations which must be made before applicants receive certification and are allowed the freedom of the planet. It has been requested that you be told – not all will be accepted. Those who are not will be returned to the ship."

Kishara shivered, and there was a general mutter of dismay and one question, shouted from elsewhere on the ship.

"What then, Pilots? Are we returned to the mercies of the homeworld?"

Pilot ven'Deelin raised a hand, and Kishara marked that it was not entirely steady.

"The pilots – by which I mean myself and my copilot, and the pilot-sets from the other two transports – will be discussing our options. I believe that we may still do better for you than the homeworld, but we have not the details, having only been made aware of this within the last hour ourselves."

She paused, perhaps ready to receive other questions. None came. She inclined her head and continued.

"We have received a protocol from the Colonization Office. Tablet holders will find this on their screens. Please share it with your group. The first call for this ship is expected within the next hour, local."

She sighed and closed her eyes briefly.

"Are there other questions?"

There were none. The pilot inclined her head.

"Tablet holders, please choose one of yours to pick up rations for the groups at the distribution point."

The screen went dark. Pritti used her chin to point at the man sitting two seats to her left.

"Tai Lor, of your goodness, fetch our rations."

* * *

Their group was among the last to be called to the shuttle to go down to the planet surface.

The ten that remained of their original pod of twelve sat in their designated area. Once they were strapped in Pritti, tablet in hand, read out their personal names one by one: Kishara, Mor Gan, Elasa, Tai Lor, Peiaza, Jas Min, Wilcee, Bri And, Kanni, ending with her own.

"What sort of examinations do you think we will be given?" ask Elasa, who looked the veriest child.

"Physical, certainly," said Bri And.

"Will they take note of our gifts?" asked Wilcee. "Have they even been told of our gifts?"

"Surely so," said Jas Min. "How could *that* have been hidden?"

"Very easily," answered Wilcee. "One need only fail of mentioning it."

"That would be unscrupulous," Jas Min objected, which drew a laugh from Peiaza.

"Recall who made these pleasant arrangements on our behalf," she said.

"Certainly, the Dragon is honorable, in its way," Jas Min said, "but if you would have it otherwise, what do you say of the Rabbit?"

"That they lend credence to the Dragon's actions," came the response. "And that it is entirely possible that *they* have not been given the whole, no more than we were."

"Well, if you – " Jas Min began, but Pritti waved a hand, cutting his comment short.

"The information included here," she raised her tablet so that all might see it, "is that the Colonization Office is fully informed regarding our situation and our abilities. They have no objection to talents of any sort. It is stated that some number of the existing population are likewise gifted."

She lowered the tablet and frowned.

"If I read this aright," she continued, "we comprise a second wave of colonists, the first having lost many due to the *unusual environment which favors a particular sensitivity, and also the complete absence of sensitivity.*"

"So some of us," said Tai Lor lightly, "may be found too little in tune – or too much in tune – with this unusual environment? Which is it, I wonder?"

"That will be made known to us soon enough, I'll wager," said Peiaza, in a tone that predicted such knowledge to be dire.

The rest of them exchanged glances.

"I, for one, will put off worry until we are landed, tested, and presented with real information," Bri And said sensibly. "In the meanwhile, I shall be taking a nap."

Despite they passed the entire journey unaware, that state had been more exhausting than restful. Kishara found that she might also welcome a nap. She disposed herself more comfortably in her chair, leaned her head back into the rest, and closed her eyes.

* * *

Kishara shivered in the damp breeze that teased them as they moved slowly, one-by-one, down the ramp to the omnibus at the far end. For all it was damp, and cooler than her jacket allowed for, Kishara approved of the breeze. Its freshness woke her senses, and sharpened her thoughts. There was a quality to it – a sort of sparkle, as one might have in a glass of mineral water.

The port beyond the bus – was meager. One of course had not expected Solcintra, but had envisioned something nearer to one of the modest outworld ports that *Maplekai* served.

From her vantage near the top of the ramp, she saw that she had been optimistic in her imaginings. The port was possibly three streets deep, and three long. Most of the buildings were low, only one rising above four stories, and that so much higher that it must be the portmaster's office.

Well, she said to herself, it is a colony world. You did *know* that.

The breeze buffeted her once more, and she wished for a heavier jacket. Pritti, ahead of her in line, shivered, and hunched her shoulders, as if that might protect her from the wind.

Kishara looked down the ramp toward the bus – and frowned.

A woman wearing a green tunic, and holding a clipboard, stood at the door of the bus. Each person had to speak with her before they were allowed to board the bus. And, as Kishara watched, here came Pritti, tablet in hand.

Kishara frowned, and tried to look away, to look at Pritti just ahead of her in line, but her eyes would not move; she was wholly concentrated on the scene at the door.

The woman in the green tunic held out her hand. Pritti, clutching the tablet tight, spoke – sharply, so it seemed to Kishara. The official spoke again, extending her hand more fully, and after a moment's hesitation, Pritti surrendered the tablet.

Kishara, watching, leaned forward even as Pritti turned to board the bus. In that instant, her eyesight blurred, she stumbled – and felt her arm caught, steadying her.

"Here now!" a voice said sharply. "What's amiss?"

Kishara drew a shaky breath, and turned her head. It was grim-faced Bri And who was her rescuer.

"I came a bit dizzy," she said, trying to ignore the phantoms obscuring her vision. It was as if she trying to focus on his face from a distance, with a bright, busy crowd between them. She took another breath.

"Perhaps there's something in the air," she said.

Bri And sniffed.

"The more likely cause is too little food. Even entranced, we burn calories, and we burned more than were replenished by ration bars and that wretched drink. Haven't you noticed that we're all thin as needles?"

The line moved forward a few paces. Bri And stepped to her side, still holding her arm, keeping her steady. It was impertinence, perhaps, but she was grateful for his support.

Kishara took another breath and closed her eyes briefly, to no avail. The busy crowd still bustled behind her eyelids, sharper now that reality did not distract her.

"Mind your step," Bri And said from that distant reality. "We are going more quickly now."

She opened her eyes and moved at his urging, allowing him still to support her, while she kept her head bent and concentrated on seeing the ramp through the phantom crowds.

At last, they stood on hard crete behind Pritti, who had just reached the guard in her green tunic.

"Name," she stated, and Pritti murmured a reply, shoulders hunched.

Kishara's vision cleared, the scene in front of her taking on more weight. Surely, she had seen this – only very recently? Frowning, she inched closer, and Bri And came with her, firm hand under her elbow.

The woman in the green tunic had made her note on the clipboard, and held out a broad hand, palm up.

"Tablet," she said.

Pritti stiffened, and clutched the tablet closer.

"I am the guide for the remaining ten of us. The pilots entrusted me with the duty, to care for the group and impart such information as the tablet provides."

"Yes," the guard said, barely patient. "That duty has come to an end. All of you are equally under the care and protection of the Office of

Colonization Services. The tablets are to be returned to the ship. The pilots have said it."

Yes, Kishara thought. This was precisely what she had seen from the top of the ramp, replaying now, in real time. She recalled the Healer who had tried so hard to argue her a Seer. Had he been right, after all? But what had increased her gift to the point where the future overwrote her present? Was this what it was like for Seers – no. She brought herself up. No, the Healer had said something, had *shown* her something, that she had scarcely been able to grasp at the time. She groped for the memory while Pritti bowed her head, and placed the tablet into the guard's waiting hand.

The guard jerked her head toward the bus, and Pritti, shoulders drooping, turned and climbed the stairs.

The guard turned aside to place the tablet into a box.

"You now," Bri And murmured, and supported Kishara as she stepped forward, concentrating on her surroundings – the carpeted stairs into the bus, the red exterior, the guard's green tunic, and the emblems on each shoulder. The ghosts of the future still crowded at the edge of her sight, but if she held her attention firm, they did not, much, disrupt reality.

The guard turned back, hefting her clipboard, a frown forming on her angular face.

"What's this, then?"

Kishara swallowed, but no words came, all of her resources concentrated on holding the ghosts at bay.

"She feels unwell," Bri And said after a moment. "Rations were short."

The guard's face softened somewhat.

"Understood," she said. "Name?"

Kishara found her tongue, "Kishara jit'Luso."

The guard made a tick-mark on her clipboard, and raised her eyes to Bri And.

"Name?"

"Bri And bel'Vester," he said.

The guard again had recourse to her clipboard, and jerked her head toward the bus.

"Please board. There will be food and a physician at the examination hall."

They passed on, Kishara more than glad of Bri And's support on the stairs. Inside, there were only a few seats left open. He saw her situated on the first they found, near the center of the bus.

"Sit and be easy," he murmured. "If you wish it, I will be your support when we debark."

"Thank you," she answered, and managed a polite inclination of her head. "I am steadier than I was."

That earned her a sharp look, but there was another passenger moving up the aisle, and perforce Bri And moved on, to a seat in the back of the bus.

Kishara sighed, leaned back in her seat, and closed her eyes.

This was a mistake. The ghosts of might-be assaulted her. She saw, in an ever-increasing cascade the bus exploding, bodies falling to the street, blood bright against the stones, windows smashed, and ships lifting willy-nilly from port. She saw a body in an airlock, a catch-net floating against a backdrop of stars, a plate of bread and cheese, the sharp-faced individual she had seen in shipboard dreaming, and another explosion as glass flew and pierced her.

She cried out at that, but the visions flowed on. She saw Pritti lift her hand, and have her silver ring off; she saw the guard in the green tunic pulling a side arm from her belt, and offering it, butt-first, across her arm. She saw people, a busload of people, fall and lie still. She saw – she saw –

A stinging slap to her cheek shocked her eyes open. The guard, without her clipboard now, was bending over, her bulk shielding Kishara from the rest of the bus.

"What is it?" the woman demanded.

"I see – disaster, murder, and mayhem," Kishara heard herself say, well aware that it was babble and the guard would think her mad. "The bus explodes, there are bodies in the street. I am struck, and we are robbed – "

The guard placed a hand on Kishara's shoulder and pressed, not unkindly. Kishara's voice died, and she felt considerably calmer. The guard inclined her head, looking both wise and sad.

"I see," she said. "You will be going back to the ships, my dear. The world is too much for you."

Kishara blinked up at her.

"*Is* it the air?" she asked.

"In a manner of speaking. It takes some harder than others, and the lesson we have from the first wave is that those it takes hardest cannot survive. The ambient conditions will tear your mind apart, and you'll become a danger to yourself and your neighbors. Best for all and everyone, to go back where you came from."

"Never that," Kishara snapped, and the woman lifted a shoulder.

"Go someplace else, then, but the Office won't let you stay here. For this moment, I can offer you a drug that will put you to sleep – "

But Kishara had had enough of being put to sleep for her own good.

"I thank you," she said coldly, "but no. I seem calm enough now."

"That's because I'm shielding you," the guard told her. "Once I take my hand away, those sights will come back again. Unless you shield yourself."

Kishara took a breath.

"I have seen danger to this bus and passengers," she said as calmly as she could manage. "I know that this may not come to pass, but equally it may."

The guard sighed lightly, patted her shoulder and removed her hand. "I'll just fetch my kit," she said, and left.

Kishara squinted after her, ignoring the ghosts rioting at the edge of her vision. She thought she saw – no, she *did* see! – a shimmer as of bright metal or reinforced glass.

She looked across the aisle at her fellow refugees, startled to find many displaying a similar effect.

Was this, Kishara wondered, something natural that she lacked, or was it–

She almost closed her eyes, but managed to avoid that error. Instead, she concentrated on the Healer who had tried so hard to save her for the homeworld. He had hurriedly attempted to teach her something that she had not been able to grasp, or even imagine. Blind and ignorant, she had tried to follow his instructions, and had failed.

Now, however, with the ambient conditions assisting her, she understood. In memory, she could even hear the Healer's voice, patiently telling over the steps for building a shield around her core.

Concentrating, Kishara used her new understanding to follow those careful, remembered instructions.

She felt heat at the base of her spine, which the Healer had mentioned as a sign that she was engaged with her gifts. The ghosts at the edge of her vision went into a frenzy, but she forced herself to concentrate on the shadow that was building about her, which was becoming more solid, despite the shadow's attempts to distract and dismay –

There was a *click*, surely audible to the rest of the bus. The ghosts were gone. It was – quiet inside her head, though she had not been aware of any noise until it had stopped.

"You might have done that first," said a familiar voice, and Kishara looked up into the face of the guard, who had a small medkit in her hand.

The woman smiled slightly.

"That's what you want, though I'll tell you right now that, shielded or open, the Office still isn't likely to let you stay."

Kishara sighed, thinking of those possible futures that had come to her attention, and inclined her head.

"Perhaps I will be able to convince them otherwise," she said, and the guard gave her a thoughtful look.

"Perhaps you will," she said, and went away toward the front of the bus.

* * *

Kishara sat quietly inside her shields, and thought about those other things the Healer had tried to teach her in their short time together. Shields, she recalled, were vital, a protection and also a secure situation to rest behind. That said, the Healer had not recommended staying entirely behind shields. The information her gifts brought to her was valuable – uniquely valuable – and she should therefore allow her shields to be somewhat open, balancing the needs for protection and information.

Resting behind her shields, she sighed and considered what else the Healer might have told her.

"Stop the bus," a clear and absolutely certain voice stated. "Everyone else, be entirely still."

The bus slowed, and stopped.

Kishara opened her eyes.

At the driver's station stood – Mor Gan, from her group, now draped in necklaces, his fingers glittering with rings. His pockets visibly bulged.

"Good," he said to the bus driver. "Give me all of your money."

The driver reached beneath the seat and produced a pouch, which he handed to Mor Gan. No one else in her sight moved. Cautiously, she turned her head very slightly to the right, seeing more passengers frozen in place.

"Give me your weapon," Mor Gan directed the bus driver, and received what seemed to be a small firearm.

"Open the door," Mor Gan said, then, having disposed pouch and gun about his person.

The driver touched something on his board and the bus door sighed open.

"Keep absolutely still," Mor Gan said and stepped into the aisle, looking over the motionless passengers with such an expression on his face, that Kishara feared for their lives.

Whatever thought had passed through his mind, Kishara saw him reject it. When he spoke, that note she had marked before was in his voice, only much clearer, issuing not suggestions but *commands*.

"All of you," he said, "go to sleep for ten minutes. When you awake, you will have forgotten me entirely."

He turned and leapt down the stairs into the street.

Kishara jumped to her feet, rushed down the aisle, and leapt the stairs in his wake. Mor Gan was racing toward a small street just beyond the back of the bus. She gave chase, thinking only that he had robbed the driver, and many passengers – and that he must be stopped. She had reached the top of the street he had vanished into before she also recalled that he had taken a gun.

She leaned into a doorway, and tried to reason her way to the path she ought to take. Going to the Office of Colonization would be fruitless; she had to believe that Mor Gan, whose gift had been the ability to *suggest* things, had found that gift enhanced. She must believe, therefore, that his suggestion that he be forgotten had taken hold, and no one on the bus, or even from their group, would recall him, never mind be alarmed by a description of his alleged crimes. Especially, she thought wryly, when that description came from the weak-minded woman who was to be sent away before the planet broke her mind.

She recalled the visions she had experienced – the bus exploding, people dying – but none of that had happened. Recall, she told herself, the Healer had said that the future is not immutable. What she had seen on the bus had been *possible* futures. Mor Gan's actions had put them onto a path where bus and passengers survived; they were past that point; it could not be chosen again.

Every subsequent choice Mor Gan made limited the number of choices he *could* make, until he was locked into one line, all his future actions forced.

At the moment, she supposed him dazzled, perhaps slightly mad, with the sudden scope of his gift. Perhaps she *should* follow him, and bring him into hand before he did someone a grievous hurt. She thought she could trust her luck to keep her safe from ... too much harm. She – no.

She was a fool.

Mor Gan had come from Low Port. He was no innocent. He was a man who profited from the pain of others. Perhaps he had chosen to emigrate because he desired a wider field for his efforts. Perhaps Low Port had become ... inhospitable to him. Why did not matter.

What did matter was that Mor Gan *meant* to do mischief, and very possibly worse. He had intended this robbery, or something like it, from the first. It was only a bonus that his power of suggestion had increased under the ambient conditions.

The question for her, however – that remained the same: How was she to stop him? Surely, it fell to her to stop him, as the only person on-planet who remembered him.

Kishara bit her lip, thinking, taking stock of her gifts, both of them. Then she nodded once. Mor Gan sealed his future as he ran, decision by decision. *She* had the advantage, there. *She* could see ahead of him, and choose the path that would allow her to stop him. Her luck – she still trusted that her luck would keep her safe in the doing of it.

She smiled slightly. All that was required of her was to chose the correct path. Now that she had the way of it, that should not be so difficult a task.

Still smiling, she opened her shields, and let the ghosts of the future take her.

* * *

She came to herself standing at the side of a table in what appeared to be a tavern. It was a noisy room, but the table her gifts had chosen for her was occupied only by a dark-haired man wearing a pilot's jacket, wineglass in hand, gaze directed at some landscape only he could see. He wore a great, glittering gaud of a ring on his unencumbered hand, and Kishara, still in thrall to her gifts, thought that he looked familiar.

He looked up, as if he had suddenly become aware that he was not alone – black eyes under strong black brows, a hard face and a secretive mouth. Kishara realized that she *had* seen him, and more than once. In her dreams, and more recently, in her plans.

One of those strong brows lifted, and Kishara bent in a slight bow. Her lips parted, and she waited with interest to hear what she might say.

"Captain yos'Phelium." Her voice was not precisely steady, her tone too low for the loud room, but he heard her. His hard mouth softened slightly.

"No," he said, his voice not hard at all. "Merely Pilot yos'Phelium."

"But a yos'Phelium is never *merely* a pilot," she returned saucily.

His laugh put the lie to the grim face and stern eyes. She glanced down, lest he see the relief in her eyes – and discovered a plate of cheese, somewhat depleted, and half a small loaf of bread. It was then that she realized that she was very hungry, indeed.

"Sit," Pilot yos'Phelium said, his voice cordial. "If you have a taste for chancy company. I was about to call for more wine. Will you join me?"

"Thank you," she said, and took the chair at his left, which put her back against the wall; the room, and especially the entry door, full in her gaze.

The server arrived in answer to the pilot's glance, received the order for two glasses of wine, and the coins that paid for all.

There was a stir behind her, and he glanced in that direction before looking to her again.

"If you were not here for the previous set, you may find the music of interest," he said courteously, as if they had been partnered at a public entertainment, on the homeworld.

There came a tootling sound, and some plucking of strings as the musicians bent to their task, and here was the server again, bearing wine and a new loaf of bread.

"Cook's gift," he said. "Crowd's thinner than her baking tonight."

"Our thanks to the cook," Kishara said with fervor, though it was scarcely her place to say it.

The server swept away, and Pilot yos'Phelium tipped his head toward the plates.

"The bread is very good," he said, "and the cheese better. I did not much care for the *akashi* fruit, but you may find otherwise. Please, make yourself free."

She smiled at him, then, with no restraint at all, and reached out to raise the glass the server had set by her hand.

"To the fullness of fortune," she proposed.

Both eyebrows quirked, but he lifted his glass willingly enough, and answered her.

"To the luck."

They drank. Kishara set her glass aside and reached to the plates. The cheese was excellent, and the bread delightful. The fruit – no, the fruit was not to her taste, either. She made another selection from among the cheeses.

Behind them, the musicians played, quietly. Kishara ate, conscious of the passage of time, as well as the warmth at the base of her spine. Mindful of the abbreviated teachings of the Healer, she had made shift to examine the futures her gift had spun from the ambient conditions, and she had – she was almost entirely certain that she had – chosen that future which provided the best chance of her continued survival with her mind intact, and provided the quickest end to Mor Gan's career.

Once she had chosen, it seemed her tendency to be fortunate had leapt into operation, moving her through the port on a mission of its own. There was some confusion at the beginning of this part of her adventure, until she realized that her part was to utterly surrender her own will and submit to being moved by the force of her gift. She had achieved the knack of it eventually, and so her feet had brought her here, to this place, to this man, and to the confrontation that would provide the solution she had chosen.

It would be soon, now, she thought. She sipped her wine, and took up another piece of bread.

She looked up to find Pilot yos'Phelium's sharp eyes on her.

"You were looking for me," he said. "*Specifically* for me."

She met his gaze calmly.

"Yes."

"Ah." He sipped wine. "I don't wish to be rude, but if there is something you need to say to me, you must speak. I'm soon away."

"Yes," she said again, and then, because in her current state she could not fail to remark them – "You have very strong shields."

"So I am told. I hope you will not ask me to lower them, for I haven't the least notion how to do so. The shields came with me into this life."

Ah, she thought, her gifts were canny, indeed.

Smiling, she inclined her head.

"My name is Kishara jit'Luso, Pilot. I am lucky, so my delm cast me out, in order that the clan take no damage from sheltering faulty genes."

He sipped his wine and considered her.

"Forgive me if I am impertinent," he said eventually, "but, being as I am, I know little of those who are gifted. It is true that my entire clan is lucky – and risky. I wonder if you put yourself in danger by seeking me out."

Danger, Kishara thought, amused.

"As the moth is endangered by the candle flame?" she asked lightly. "You are kind to regard it, but no. I think, in this moment, that our lucks reinforce each other, to the betterment of both."

"Ah?" he murmured politely.

"Yes," she said, reaching for another slice of bread with cheese. "You see, there's about to be a pirate raid."

He blinked and put his glass carefully on the table.

"A pirate raid?" he repeated.

Just then, the front door smashed open.

#

Kishara drank the last of her wine and put the glass down. It was begun; she felt the warmth at the base grow warmer still, and was content. From here ... from this moment, all was forced.

A shout went up from among the diners and drinkers, chairs and stools were noisily overturned as people leapt to their feet. Pilot yos'Phelium also rose, silently, hands loose at his sides as he observed the unfolding scene.

Kishara likewise rose, and put herself a few steps closer to his side, into the shadow of his shields.

There came another shout. A chair was thrown, a bravo ducked. Rifles were raised. Without turning around, she knew that the musicians had leapt up behind her, while, forward, the 'tender swung below the bar and came up with a long arm, oddly made, and glowing weirdly –

Pilot yos'Phelium moved, as if he would introduce himself into the situation, and put all into order. Kishara extended her hand to grip his arm tightly. He paused, and she removed her hand, for here came Mor Gan now, strolling in all unconcerned, dragging a halfling girl by her wrist.

Mor Gan had, Kishara saw, made other suggestions before his arrival into the snare of her chosen future. He now wore a space leather jacket, and at least a dozen necklaces. His hands were ablaze with rings. She felt ... something tighten around her, as if her gifts sought to protect her.

There came a sharp *fssstt!* from the weapon in the bartender's hands. The shot burned the floor near the boot of the nearest bravo, who spun, weapon up.

"Friends, friends!" Mor Gan called, his voice compelling attention. "There is no reason for dispute. We are here to pick up supplies, funds, and perhaps personnel. Please all be calm."

Even tucked inside the influence of the pilot's shields, Kishara felt drawn – a quick glance around the room showed that the bar's customers were thoroughly caught, beguiled by his voice, and entranced in a moment.

Mor Gan turned and pointed a finger at the gape-mouthed bartender.

"Put that down," he said chidingly; "you will do someone a hurt."

The bartender put the rifle on the bar.

"Very good," Mor Gan said. "Now, if you please – go to the storeroom and pack up three cases of your best liquor and wine and bring them here."

The bartender left on this mission, and Mor Gan shook the girl by the wrist, demanding to know how the weapon was disarmed. She told him, her voice flat, her face blank. Kishara frowned. The girl – surely, she had not chosen to endanger a halfling?

Mor Gan pointed to a customer seated at the bar.

"You," he said, "do as she said."

The customer rose to approach the weapon, and Mor Gan turned his attention to the room at large.

In short order, he had the entranced working for him, directing three to go among the many, who were instructed to give over all their money and precious things. This, they willingly did.

When it came their turn to donate, Kishara reached into her pocket and fingered out her entire wealth of coins. She also gave the ring she wore, looking into the collector's eyes as she did so.

His eyes were blank, as if blind. Receiving Kishara's offering, he thrust his collection tray at Pilot yos'Phelium, who deposited a few coins from an outside jacket pocket, and with not the least hesitation, drew the big gaudy ring from his finger, and placed it among the rest of the items gathered.

The collector moved past. The musicians gave their instruments, and the coins in their cup.

"Bring all that you have collected to the bar," said the compelling voice, and this, too, was done.

Kishara took a breath as Mor Gan went to the bar to inspect his takings, dragging the halfling with him. There came the subtle sound of metal ringing, loud in the silence of the room. Suddenly, he paused, and turned, holding the pilot's gaudy ring high.

"Who gave this? Raise a hand!"

Her pilot did so, blank-faced and slow, and Mor Gan came down the room toward them, ring in one hand, halfling dragged, half-stumbling in his wake.

Kishara took another breath, and tried to take comfort from the warm emanations of her gifts. This was a danger point. If Mor Gan should recognize her –

But his glance passed over her and settled on the pilot.

"Well! Pilot, is it? Jump pilot, in fact? You will be coming with me. And who is this – ah ... lady?"

He looked directly at her, no recognition in his face. Kishara, daring to look into his eyes, saw that, even as he entranced others, he was himself entranced. The guard had warned her that those who responded too well to the ambient conditions were in danger of their minds, if not their lives, and in Mor Gan's eyes Kishara saw the truth of that.

"What is your relationship with this pilot?" he asked her. "Speak true!"

"We are partners," Kishara heard herself say, flat-voiced.

"Very good. You will also be taking employment with me. What is your name?"

Her gift spoke again. "Pelli asSulo."

Mor Gan accepted the name without question.

"What is your name, Pilot? Speak true!"

"Sin Jin Isfelm," the pilot replied, lying in his turn.

"They now belong to me, as you do. Follow."

They followed, and Kishara rejoiced. They had passed a point, the quarry was trapped, and her safety assured. They *could not* vary now.

* * *

Mor Gan had designated two others besides herself and the pilot to carry his goods. He had instructed the room to forget all that had happened, and Kishara did have some curiosity as to how that would play, once they were no longer in thrall.

That, however, was not her business. Her business was to escape this planet before the ambient conditions broke her mind, and to do so in company of the Korval pilot, who was also unnaturally lucky, and safely isolated from such madness as threatened her.

Their group arrived at a shuttle, and the two extra carriers were instructed to put down their burdens. They were dismissed with a curt command to forget the events of this night.

Mor Gan then looked at his three bravos, with their blank faces and their weapons at ready, and said, "Leave me."

They went, taking their weapons with them, and Kishara spared a thought for the damage they might do on-port. Beside her, the pilot shifted, as if he were weighing this moment as an opportunity to act. She took a careful breath, and *felt* him take the decision to wait.

Excellent, she thought, he has a cool head.

Mor Gan moved then, dragging the halfling to the hatch, slapping her open palm against the plate with one hand, and with the other pushing her chin up so that the scanner registered her face and eyes.

The hatch slid open. Mor Gan snatched the halfling roughly back, slamming her into the side of the shuttle. It must have hurt, but the girl didn't cry out, nor did her expression change. She might have been a doll, Kishara thought, or a puppet. She blinked at that last thought, and wondered how deeply Mor Gan had attached the girl. If matters fell as she, Kishara, had ordered them, she would have blood on her hands if the girl were damaged, though she had not – she was certain that she had not agreed to anything that endangered an innocent.

"Stow the goods," Mor Gan snapped, and the pilot moved to do so, neither quick nor slow, face blank. Kishara picked up another case and followed him into the shuttle.

The pilot was waiting for her at the bin. He bent and breathed into her ear.

"I will want an explanation."

"No time," she answered. "Trust me."

He snorted lightly, for which she blamed him not at all, and went back out onto the dock, returning a moment later, carrying the last case. Mor Gan came after, carrying his sack of loot and shoving the halfling before him.

He slapped the switch as he passed, and the hatch came down. Kishara moved further into the shuttle to make room, which she hoped did not show too much initiative for one supposedly under Mor Gan's control. The pilot finished stowing the last crate, got the bin locked, and came after her, stopping at her side. Kishara saw him give one sharp look at the piloting board before Mor Gan arrived, striding past them toward the pilot's station.

"Sin Jin will pilot, Pelli will take the jump-seat. I will have the co-pilot's chair. My carte blanche will kneel, so."

He shoved the girl roughly to the decking. She made no protest, nor even blinked, her eyes staring blindly ahead.

Kishara sank into the jump-seat, as directed. Pilot yos'Phelium went to his appointed station, sat, and stared down at the board. For a long moment, he did nothing at all, and Kishara caught her breath. If he were to openly resist, now – well, but he couldn't, could he? They were all caught and moving toward her chosen future.

Mor Gan made a small sound, slipped a hand into his belt and withdrew a flat rectangle, which he held out. It was a ship's key, Kishara saw, though there was something odd about it—as if it had been dipped in chocolate, or –

"You will want this," Mor Gan said.

The pilot turned his head, eyes dropping to the key, but he made no other move.

"Take it," Mor Gan snapped, and Kishara felt the force of that order act on her own muscles. Her hand twitched, and she pressed it firmly against her knee.

"Dock us with the ship *Merry Mushroom*," Mor Gan said. "Do not contact them."

The pilot's hand moved slowly, but he did take the key, and pushed it into the slot. The board came live. Kishara could see that his fingers bore dark stains, and looked to the halfling, the hostage, who knelt motionless on the deck. Whose blood is on that key, she asked herself, and the pilot gave the shuttle leave to lift.

\#

Kishara felt her gifts begin to cool as the shuttle rose, and she breathed a careful sigh of relief, though it was far too soon, much could still go wrong. Perhaps, now, *even more* could go wrong. She had made her decisions, and chosen her future while bathed in the planet's ambient conditions. If they were now leaving the field's influence, then – she was safe, surely, from the two dark futures that had been hers?

"This is *Merry Mushroom*," a voice came out of the comm. "Aincha talking to me, Sinda?"

Mor Gan shoved the girl toward the board, snarling, "Talk to them. There is a situation which the pilot must attend. Say it!"

The halfling leaned forward.

"This is Jaim, Vina," she said, her voice flat. "Sinda's got a glitch to ride. We're coming in to dock."

Hesitation, then a gruff, "Come on, then."

The pilot reached to his board.

\#

"Docking complete."

The brilliant burn of her gift was embers now, leaving Kishara cold. She could remember – she could remember what she had decided, she recalled making choices, but the manner of choosing and deciding – that was lost to her. She looked to Mor Gan, but if he was experiencing the same sort of loss, there was no outward sign of it.

The halfling had wilted, her shoulders hunched, and she directed her sightless gaze now at the decking on which she knelt.

Mor Gan unsnapped his webbing, stood, and yanked the girl to her feet.

"Follow us!" he snapped, pushing ahead, and shoving the halfling before him. "Go!"

The girl went, though too slowly to please her captor. He shoved her again, and when she reached the hatch, slammed her forcefully against the wall, grabbing her wrist and jerking her hand to the plate as if he intended to rip the arm from the socket.

Kishara heard a gasp – the first the girl had made, and looked sharply. She felt a hand on her shoulder, and glanced up, to see the pilot frowning at her. He meant her to stay back, she thought, and stepped out of his way.

The hatch opened into a common room. Mor Gan threw the girl in ahead of him. She hit the deck with a cry, rolling. Crew started up with shouts, alarm showing on their faces.

"Sit down and be calm!" Mor Gan said firmly, and Kishara with a sinking heart heard that *particular* note still in his voice. She had been a fool, playing with what she did not understand. Was she a goddess, to pick and choose the future she preferred? The planet's ambient conditions did more, and worse, than magnify such gifts one possessed. It overset one's reason, and –

"Kill him!" screamed the girl on the floor. "Kill him! He killed Father and Sinda!"

It was the pilot who moved first, fast and sure. There was a snap, loud even above the shouting of the crew. The pilot took Mor Gan's weight and sank to one knee, seeing him gently to the deck, and closed his empty, staring eyes.

#

"I am," the pilot said to the question put by Jaim Evrit, daughter of Trader Ban Evrit and Pilot Sinda Mark, "Can Ith yos'Phelium."

Like the refugees, he omitted his clan affiliation, possibly, Kishara thought, because he was conversing with the clanless.

"And you, ma'am?" Jaim Evrit asked.

"Kishara jit'Luso," she answered.

The halfling nodded.

"Do either of *you* know what happened, that I could finally act on my own?"

It was well that the question was put in such a fashion, Kishara thought. She need not lie, nor confess her part in the ruin of this girl's life. Though she would have to explain herself more fully to Pilot yos'Phelium. Later. In private.

"The field is particular to the planet," Kishara said. "I felt it ebb, as we lifted."

She bit her lip, and cast a conscious look at Can Ith yos'Phelium.

"I was in the same test group," she said. "We all felt the effects as soon as we hit planet, but he –" she waved toward the lock, where the body rested – "he understood the possibilities more quickly than the others of us, and did not hesitate to act for his own advantage."

Can Ith inclined his head, and Kishara awaited the next reasonable question, from him, or from some one of the crew, but the first mate – a grey-haired woman called Vina Greiz – spoke then, and at a tangent.

"All well and good," she said. "*My* question is what we're gonna do now. Trader's gone, pilot, too. Young Jaim –" She threw a worried look at the halfling slumped in her chair.

"I'm not certified," Jaim said, and her voice was stronger. She straightened. "Can't run the trade."

"We'll have to marry *Shroom* to the Mikancy Family," said another of the crew from the back.

"No." Young Jaim's face was set.

"What else then?" came yet a third voice. "Sell out and stay downside?"

"Not that either." Jaim took a hard breath and gave Can Ith a stare.

"You're a Jump pilot."

He glanced down at the gaudy ring, rescued from the sack of stolen goods and back on his finger.

"That is so," he admitted.

"Are you at liberty?" she asked then, and he smiled.

"Very much so."

"I was raised in a trading house," Kishara said, for the ship had lost two skills this day. Both must be replaced, if Jaim was determined to keep her independence. "I can advise, as required. I think that you will not need to marry to your disadvantage."

Jaim's smile was grim as she looked over her crew.

"I'm family," she said. "I *can* offer contract."

Kishara bowed, and so did Pilot Can Ith.

"I think we might manage," Jaim said to her crew. "And not impossible to borrow a Second Trader from one of our friendlies, if we gotta."

"We trust *them*?" the first mate demanded, jerking her head in the direction of themselves.

"You'd rather the Mikancy?" Jaim asked, sharp and strong. "You know their style. We'll be lucky to be set down on a back world alive. These two gentles have done more good for this ship an' crew in one day than the Mikancy in all the decades we've known 'em."

The crew was silent. The first mate threw up her hands.

"We trust 'em, then. What's next?"

"Gotta cover the route," Jaim said, and stood. "Need to get goin.'"

"In that wise," Can Ith said slowly. "Let us first make up a pod, with the stolen goods, and our late friend, and a locator. We will inform the port authority before we Jump out."

"Yes," said Jaim, and looked again to the first mate.

"Vina, show Pilot Can Ith to his seat, please. Trader Kishara and me'll go over the route and the inventory."

"Right," Vina said, and turned to the rest of the crew.

"Well?" she demanded, "I don't guess you lot have stations to man, do you?"

There was a general bustle at that, and Can Ith leaned over to speak into Kishara's ear.

"And when will you tell me – only me – the rest of the truth, Kishara?"

"Soon," she told him, and smiled. "We'll have some amount of time together."

Mobile eyebrows rose.

"Will we?" he said, his head went up at the sound of his name. "A moment," he told the first mate, and looked again to Kishara.

"I look forward to our continued association," he said, politely. "Until soon."

Kishara closed her eyes in relief, feeling only tired, her gifts quiescent or dead, it mattered not one whit to her.

"Yes," she murmured. "Until soon."

* * *

They were both due leave on Fussbudget, and had agreed to share a meal at a town-side tavern not much frequented by their shipmates.

It was there that she finally told him the tale entire, stinting her part not at all.

" ... so they were right – the Council," Kishara concluded, putting down her glass. "We *are* an unpredictable menace, and a danger to the innocent."

Can Ith did not immediately answer, but she was used to his ways by now, and did not suppose his silence signaled either condemnation or approval. He was thinking, that was all. In a moment – or a day – he would come forth with what thought had produced.

The product of thought came just after he set his own glass on the table.

"The Council was wrong," he stated, his voice allowing no room for doubt. "No one of the small talents, saving those who had already set themselves up to be a danger and a menace, were a threat to society or to the homeworld. Some few may have been dangers to themselves, and might have harmed an innocent through inexperience, or error."

He glanced at her. She motioned him to go on.

"The Council would have done better for all and everyone had they allowed the Healers to amend their charter, and enlarge their House. They would have done no particular harm, had they granted the small talents their own Guild. From there, the Guilds might have assisted each other, to the betterment of both, and to have a Talent in the clan would have been a matter of pride."

He met her eyes.

"Ambient conditions came into play when the game was removed from Liad, and untrained persons were left to fend for themselves. Then and *only then* did some few of the small talents become dangerous, and that not from their own desires." He moved his shoulders and raised a hand to call for more wine.

"Well. We must allow the account to show that one was not so well-intentioned as he might have been."

"Two," Kishara said. "I abetted murder and mind control, stole your life –"

Can Ith blinked.

"Is this pride?" he interrupted, black eyes well-opened.

"It is not, and you well know it!"

"Will you strip Mor Gan's honors from him? I do assure you, he *meant* to rob, and to kill, and to control. Do not imagine, my friend, that he was a good man made bad by your meddling with futures."

"No, of course he was not – " Kishara began, and paused as the server came to refresh their glasses.

"As for having stolen my life – " Can Ith said, as soon as the server had left them – "that attempt had been made, and I decided upon my answer before ever you stopped at my table." He raised his glass, black eyes quizzing her over the rim.

"Now, answer me this. Can you be certain that *your* luck was ascendant?"

She blinked.

"What do you mean?"

He grinned.

"Korval is lucky – that is well-known. Does it not make sense to suppose that ambient conditions acted upon my own gift, as well as yours? Who, in fact, meddled with whom, and for what gain?"

He sipped, and put the glass down. Kishara continued to stare.

"But your shields – "

He snorted. "My shields have never protected me from the action of Korval's luck before. I see no reason why it should have been otherwise under ambient conditions."

He leaned forward, catching her gaze with his.

"Do you not see how *neat* it all is? That a ship should discover an urgent need for a Jump pilot just as I had decided to walk away from my clan and make my own future? *That* is how my luck works, Kishara. *I* think that your luck operated to preserve you by placing you into the shadow of mine, which was already engaged. There was risk; your life might have been forfeit, but we chanced upon a best case for both."

He leaned back, picked up his glass, and waited.

She took a hard breath.

"That's – eerie," she said at last.

"Yes," he agreed, smiling. He raised his glass. "A toast."

She lifted her her glass.

"To ambient conditions," Can Ith said, "and to our very good fortunes."

About the Authors

Maine-based writers Sharon Lee and Steve Miller teamed up in the late 1980s to bring the world the story of Kinzel, an inept wizard with a love of cats, a thirst for justice, and a staff of true power.

Since then, the husband-and-wife team have written dozens of short stories and twenty-plus novels, most set in their star-spanning, nationally-bestselling Liaden Universe®.

Before settling down to the serene and stable life of a science fiction and fantasy writer, Steve was a traveling poet, a rock-band reviewer, reporter, and editor of a string of community newspapers.

Sharon, less adventurous, has been an advertising copywriter, copy editor on night-side news at a small city newspaper, reporter, photographer, and book reviewer.

Both credit their newspaper experiences with teaching them the finer points of collaboration.

Steve and Sharon are jointly the recipients of the E. E. "Doc" Smith Memorial Award for Imaginative Fiction (the Skylark), one of the oldest awards in science fiction. In addition, their work has won the much-coveted Prism Award (*Mouse and Dragon* and *Local Custom*), as well as the Hal Clement Award for Best Young Adult Science Fiction (*Balance of Trade*), and the Year's Best Military and Adventure SF Readers' Choice Award ("Wise Child").

Sharon and Steve passionately believe that reading fiction ought to be fun, and that stories are entertainment.

Steve and Sharon maintain a web presence at korval.com

Novels by Sharon Lee & Steve Miller

The Liaden Universe®

Fledgling

Saltation

Mouse and Dragon

Ghost Ship

Dragon Ship

Necessity's Child

Trade Secret

Dragon in Exile

Alliance of Equals

The Gathering Edge

Neogenesis

Accepting the Lance

Trader's Leap

Omnibus Editions

The Dragon Variation

The Agent Gambit

Korval's Game

The Crystal Variation

Story Collections

A Liaden Universe Constellation: Volume 1

A Liaden Universe Constellation: Volume 2

A Liaden Universe Constellation: Volume 3

A Liaden Universe Constellation: Volume 4

The Fey Duology

Duainfey

Longeye

Gem ser'Edreth

The Tomorrow Log

Novels by Sharon Lee

The Carousel Trilogy

Carousel Tides

Carousel Sun

Carousel Seas

Jennifer Pierce Maine Mysteries

Barnburner

Gunshy

THANK YOU

Thank you for your support of our work.

Sharon Lee and Steve Miller

Made in the USA
Las Vegas, NV
17 April 2021